This Walker book belongs to:

_____

_____

_____

First published 1984 by Julia MacRae Books

This edition published 2014 by Walker Books Ltd
87 Vauxhall Walk, London SE11 5HJ

7 9 10 8

This book has been typeset in Plantin

Printed in China

British Library Cataloguing in Publication Data:
a catalogue record for this book is available from the British Library

ISBN 978-1-4063-5641-0

www.walker.co.uk

Willy the Wimp

Anthony Browne

WALKER BOOKS

AND SUBSIDIARIES

LONDON • BOSTON • SYDNEY • AUCKLAND

Willy wouldn't hurt a fly.

Willy worried about stepping on
tiny insects every time he went
for a walk. When someone knocked
into him, he always said,
"Oh, I'm sorry!"
Even when it wasn't his fault.

Sometimes when he was out walking,
the suburban gorilla gang bullied him.
"Oh, I'm sorry!" said Willy
when they hit him.
    The suburban gorillas called him
Willy the Wimp.

Willy hated that name. Willy the Wimp!

One evening when Willy was reading his comic, he saw . . .

That sounds just the thing for me, thought
Willy. So he sent some money to the
address in the advertisement.

He rushed to the door every morning
to catch the postman. "Oh, I'm sorry!"
said Willy when the postman brought
nothing for him.

But one day a package arrived . . .

This was it! Willy opened it excitedly.
Inside was a book: it told Willy
what to do . . .

First some exercises.

Then some jogging.

Willy had to go on a special diet.

He went to aerobics classes
where everybody danced to
disco music. Willy felt a bit silly.

And he went to a body-building club.

Willy took up weight lifting, and gradually over
weeks and months Willy got bigger . . . and bigger . . .

and bigger . . .

AND BIGGER!

Willy looked in the mirror.
He liked what he saw.

So when Willy walked down the street

and saw the suburban gorillas attacking Millie . . .

They ran.

"Oh . . . Willy," said Millie.

"What, Millie?" said Willy.

"You're my hero, Willy," said Millie.

"Oh . . . Millie," said Willy.

Willy was proud.

"I'm not a wimp!"

A hero.

BANG!

"Oh, I'm sorry!" said Willy.